Jungle Tales

p

This book belongs to

Contents

Monkey
Mayhem

Mickey and Maxine Monkey had
finished breakfast and were rushing
off to play.

"Be careful!" called their mum.
"And DON'T make too much noise!"

"Okay" the cheeky monkeys promised.

8

"WHEEEE,"
screeched Mickey.

"WA-HOOOO!"
hollered Maxine.

The noise echoed through the whole jungle—
Mickey and Maxine just couldn't be quiet!

9

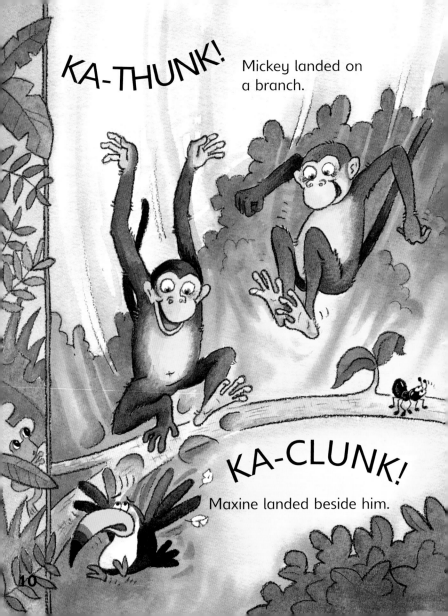

KA-THUNK!

Mickey landed on a branch.

KA-CLUNK!

Maxine landed beside him.

10

KER-AACK!

"OOOHHH NOOOO!"

the monkeys hollered as the branch snapped in two.

"YI-I-IKES!"

they shrieked, as they went tumbling down, down, down.

11

KERITHUMMPP!
SPROI-OI-OING!

The jungle shook as the two monkeys crashed to the ground, then sprang to their feet. "YIPPPEEEEEE!" the monkeys cheered, brushing themselves off.

"That was so much **FUN!**" exclaimed Maxine. "Let's go get Chico Chimp and see if he wants to do it, too!"

Chattering as they went, the two monkeys scrambled back up to the tree tops.

"HEY, CHICO! COME AND PLAY WITH US!" they bellowed as they swung through the branches towards the chimps' house.

All through the jungle, animals shook their heads and covered their ears. Couldn't anyone keep those naughty, noisy monkeys quiet?

Chico Chimp was soon ready to play with his friends. The three of them had a great time swinging, tumbling, and bouncing together. Then they spotted a coconut palm.

"Hey!" shouted Chico. "Let's get some coconuts!"

"Great!" said Maxine. "Last one up the tree is a rotten banana!"

17

But before they got to the tree, Grandpa Gorilla stopped them. He glared at them.

"**Clear off,** you mischief-makers," he said. "You've given everyone enough headaches for one day. My grandson Gulliver is asleep by the river, and if you wake him up, I will be very, very upset!"

"Sorry," whispered Maxine, looking down at the ground. Everyone in the jungle knew it was a big mistake to upset Grandpa Gorilla!

"We'll be quiet," the three friends promised.

19

Mickey, Maxine and Chico started to wander away. Then Mickey said, "Let's just just climb the tree. Maybe we can do that quietly."

"Okay," the others agreed half-heartedly.

"It's better than doing nothing," said Maxine.

From their perch up among the coconuts, the three friends could see out over the whole jungle.

They saw Jerome Giraffe teaching his son Jeremy to nibble leaves...

...and they saw Portia Parrot giving her daughter Penelope her first flying lesson.

And right below them, they saw Gulliver Gorilla sleeping peacefully by the river.

And... uh-oh! They saw something else, too. Claudia Crocodile was nearby. She was snapping her big, sharp teeth – and heading straight for Gulliver!

The three friends didn't think twice. Maxine shouted,

"GET UP, GULLIVER!

GET UP RIGHT NOOOOWW!"

At the same time, Mickey and Chico began throwing coconuts at Claudia.

THWAACKK!

went the coconuts.

SMAACCCKK!

they went, right on Claudia's hard crocodile head.

"OWW-WOOWW!"

moaned Claudia.

"OWW-WOW OWW-WOW!"

"What's going on here?" Grandpa Gorilla shouted up into the coconut tree. "I thought I told you three to keep quiet!"

All the noise woke Gulliver. The little gorilla sat up, looked around, and ran to his grandpa, who was hurrying towards the river.

Then he saw Claudia swimming away, and he realised what had happened. He grabbed Gulliver and gave him a great big gorilla hug. "I'm so glad you're safe!" he said.

Maxine, Mickey and Chico came down from the tree.

"Sorry about the noise," Chico said.

By this time all the other gorillas had gathered round, and so had most of the other jungle animals.

"What's all the commotion about?" asked Jerome Giraffe.

"Yes, what's going on?" squawked Portia Parrot.

"These three youngsters are heroes," said Grandpa. "They saved my grandson from being eaten by Claudia Crocodile!"

Everyone cheered, and Mrs Monkey and Mrs Chimp beamed with pride.

"You deserve a reward," said Grandpa Gorilla. "And I think your reward should be..."

All the other animals held their breath.

PEEEEE!"

cheered Mickey, Maxine and Chico.
Their grins were almost as wide
as the river.

"OH,
NOOOOOO!"

all the other animals groaned together—
but they were all smiling, too.

Gym Giraffe

Jeremy Giraffe loved going out with his dad to gather the juicy green leaves for their dinner.

"This is where the most delicious leaves are," said Dad, reaching w-a-a-a-y UP. to a very high branch.
"Remember the tallest trees have the tastiest leaves, and the tiny top leaves are the tenderest!"

37

One morning, Jeremy decided it was time to gather leaves on his own.

"The tallest trees have the tastiest leaves," he whispered to himself, "and the tiny top leaves are the tenderest."

Jeremy stopped at a very tall tree and looked up. There at the top were some tiny, tender, tasty-looking leaves.

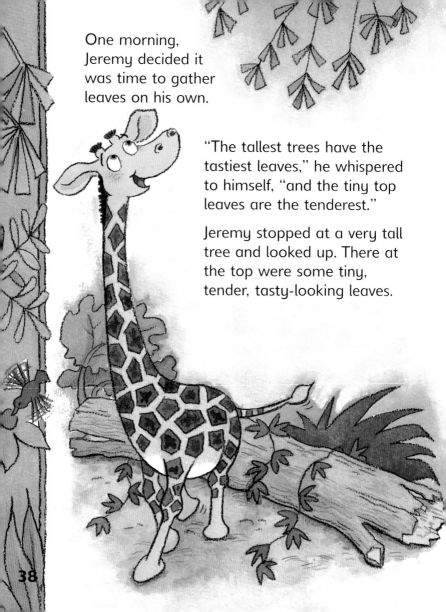

Stre - e - e - e - e - etching
his neck just as he had seen his dad do, Jeremy
reached as high as he could. It wasn't very high!

"Oh, no," he thought. "How will
I reach the tiny, tasty top leaves if
my neck won't stretch?"

So Jeremy went back home with his neck hanging down in despair.

"Why, Jeremy, what's wrong?" asked his mum. When Jeremy told her, she gave his neck a nuzzle.

"Your neck's still growing," she assured him.
"Eat your greens and get lots of sleep, and you'll
soon be able to reach the tastiest, tenderest
leaves on the tallest trees in the jungle!"

41

That afternoon, Jeremy went out to try again.

Portia Parrot saw Jeremy struggling to reach the top of the tree. Trying to be helpful, she swooped down and plucked a few of the tenderest leaves for him.

When Portia gave Jeremy the leaves, his spots went pale with shame and embarrassment.

"I should be able to get those myself," he wailed. "Why won't my neck stretch?"

"Oh, Jeremy," said Portia, "your neck is just fine! Keep eating your greens and getting lots of sleep, and it will grow!"

"But I can't wait," Jeremy insisted. "Isn't there anything I can do to stretch my neck now?"

"Perhaps there is," said Portia, thoughtfully. "Follow me!"

43

Portia led Jeremy through the jungle to a clearing. Jeremy's eyes widened with wonder at what he saw. There was so much going on!

Seymour Snake was wrapping himself round a fallen tree trunk. "Hello, Jeremy," he hissed.

"Jussssst doing my sssssslithering exercisesssss!"

Emma, Ellen and Eric Elephant were hoisting logs.

"Hi, Jeremy," they called. "This is our trunk-strengthening workout!"

In the river, Claudia Crocodile was breaking thick branches in half.

"Just limbering up my jaw muscles," she snapped.

Leonard Lion was taking his cubs, Louis and Lisa, through their pouncing paces. "Welcome to the Jungle Gym!" he called.

47

A few minutes later, Grandpa Gorilla and Leonard Lion came to greet Jeremy. "What can we do for you?" they asked.

"Can you help me stretch my neck?" asked Jeremy. "I want to be able to reach the tasty, tiny, tender leaves."

"You're still growing," said Leonard Lion. "You just have to eat your greens and get lots of sleep."

48

Jeremy's face fell, until Grandpa Gorilla said, "But we help things along with some special neck-stretching exercises. Come with us!"

Grandpa got Jeremy started right away.
"S-t-r-e-t-c-h to the left!

S-t-r-e-t-c-h to the right!"
Grandpa Gorilla shouted.

"Left!
Right!
Left!
Right!"

50

"Chin lifts next," said Leonard Lion.

Jeremy s-t-r-e-e-e-t-c-h-e-d his neck to reach the branch.

"Come on, you can do it!" Portia said, cheering him on.

51

Grandpa Gorilla told Jeremy to lie down. Then he called Seymour Snake. "Start slithering!" he said.

"Aaaakkk!

gasped Jeremy, as
Seymour wrapped himself
round his neck.

"Not so tight," said Grandpa.

"That's better!" said Jeremy,
as Seymour slithered along,
pu-u-u-l-l-ing his neck muscles.

53

All the exercise made Jeremy hungry.

At supper, he had three B|G helpings of greens.

54

He was tired, too, so he went to bed early and slept soundly.

Jeremy loved the Jungle Gym and couldn't wait to go back. He went every day for the next few weeks.

After his workout each day,
Jeremy ate a good supper.

"Exercising makes me soooo
hungry..." he said.

"... and soooo

tired," he yawned,
as he fell asleep.

57

The next time, Jeremy and his dad went out
leaf-gathering together, Jeremy spotted
some succulent, sweet-looking leaves right
at the top of a tall tree.

"I'm going to get those," he said.

"They're so high up!" said Dad.

Jeremy didn't hear him. He was too busy stretching... and

stre-e-e-e-etching...

and... s t r e e e t c h i n g...

...until he stretched right up to the very top branch!

"I've done it, Dad!" he cried happily. "The exercises worked!"

59

That night, Jeremy's mum and dad made a super-special salad with the leaves Jeremy had picked.

"Was it the exercises, Jeremy?" his dad asked. "Or has your neck grown because of all the greens you've been eating and all the sleep you've been getting?"

"I don't know," replied Jeremy.

60

"I don't think it matters," said his Mum. "What matters is that you have a fine, strong, long neck that any giraffe would be proud of!"

"And I am!" said Jeremy, taking another mouthful of tasty, tender leaves. He chewed the leaves extra thoroughly— because he knew they had a very long way to go!

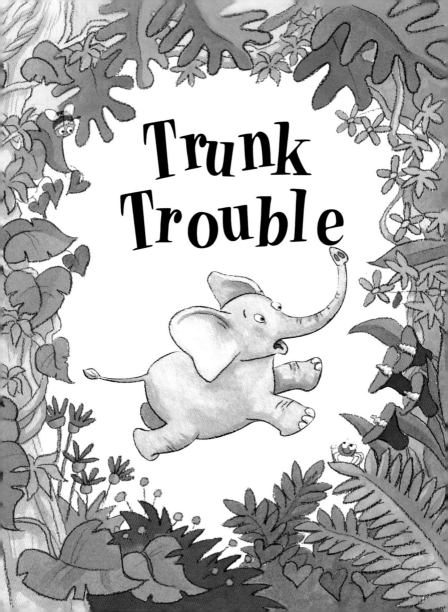

Trunk
Trouble

Emma, Ellen and Eric Elephant had spent nearly all day at the river, splashing and sploshing in the cool, clear water and giving each other excellent elephant showers.

But now it was nearly dinner time, and their rumbling tummies told them it was time to head for home.

65

First the little elephants had to dry themselves off. They made their way out to the clearing, and carefully dusted themselves with fine earth and sand.

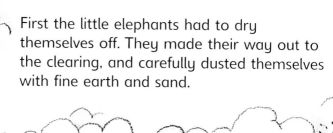

WHOOSH! WHOOSH! PUFFLE!

went Ellen with her trunk.

PUFFLE! PUFFLE! WHOOSH!

went Emma with her trunk. Both sisters had long, graceful trunks, and they were very proud of them.

WHOOSH! PUFFLE! WHOOSH... PUFF!

went Eric, when
his sisters' backs were turned.

COUGH! COUGH!

AH-CHOO!

went Emma and Ellen.
"Hey! Cut it out!" they
shouted.

Eric just giggled. He loved annoying his sisters.

67

"I'll race you home!" Eric called, when they were all dry. "Last one back is an elephant egg!" And he loped back into the jungle.

Ellen and Emma ran after him. "We'll get there first! We'll beat you!" they cried, going as quickly as they could.

Ellen and Emma were running so fast and trying so hard to catch up that they forgot to look where they were going.

All at once, Emma's feet got caught in a vine, and she lost her balance.

"Oh-oh-OOOOHHHH!" she cried as she slipped and staggered.

"Grab my trunk!" Ellen cried, reaching out to her.

71

But Emma grabbed her sister's trunk so hard that she pulled Ellen down with her. As the two elephants struggled to straighten up, their trunks got twisted together in a great big tangle.

"Help!" they cried. "Eric! Help!"

Their brother came bounding back.

"Don't worry!" he called. "I'll save you!"

Eric reached out with his trunk to try to help his sisters up. But the vine leaves were very slippery, and as he grabbed his sisters' trunks, he slipped and lost his balance, too. Now Eric's trunk was all tangled up with Emma's and Ellen's!

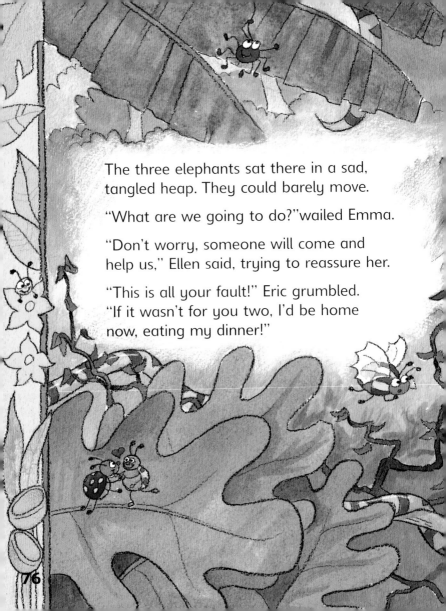

The three elephants sat there in a sad, tangled heap. They could barely move.

"What are we going to do?" wailed Emma.

"Don't worry, someone will come and help us," Ellen said, trying to reassure her.

"This is all your fault!" Eric grumbled. "If it wasn't for you two, I'd be home now, eating my dinner!"

A moment later, Seymour Snake came slithering by.

"Greetingsss," he hissed, looking curiously at the heap of elephants.

"Isss thisss an interesting new game?"

"No!" sobbed Emma. "We're all tangled together and we can't get up. Can you help us, Seymour?"

"Well I'll certainly do my bessst."

said Seymour.

"Let's see if I can untwissst you,"

He wriggled in amongst the tangle of trunks to see what he could do.

79

But everything was so muddled and jumbled together that Seymour couldn't even find his way out!

"GRACIOUSSS ME!"

he exclaimed.

"I SSSEEM TO BE SSSSTUCK!"

80

"Well, that's just great!" said Eric. "As if we didn't have enough problems — now we have a snake to worry about, too!"

"I sssuggest you sssstart thinking about a ssssolution to all thissss," Seymour hissed, "I'm not too tangled up to give you a nasssty nip!"

81

Just then Mickey and Maxine Monkey came swinging through the branches.

"HEY, YOU GUYS!"

they shouted. They weren't very far away– Mickey and Maxine always shouted.

"WHAT'S GOING ON?"

"We're stuck!" cried Ellen.
"Please help us get untangled so we can go home!"

"Well, we can try pulling you apart," said Maxine,
scurrying down. "Mickey, you take a tail, and I'll
take some ears."

83

Mickey grabbed hold of Eric's tail and Maxine gripped Ellen's ears. Then they both pulled and pulled and

p–u–l–l–e–d.

"OUCH!"

cried Eric.

"OUCH-OUCH-OOUUCCHH!"

bellowed Ellen.

"I'm being ssssqueezzzed breathlesssss!" hissed Seymour in alarm.

Mickey and Maxine gave up. Pulling clearly wasn't going to work.

Suddenly there was a flapping up above as Portia Parrot and her daughter Penelope landed in a tree. They had something in their beaks, and as everyone looked up, they let it go. A large cloud of dry, dusty, earth drifted down.

"Cough-cough-ca-choooo!"

spluttered Mickey and Maxine.

"Cough-cough-ca-choooo!"

thundered the elephants.

At first, they didn't know what had happened.
Then they realised— they had sneezed
themselves apart!

87

"Thank you," cried the elephants and Seymour.

"Happy to help!" said Portia.

"Everyone's invited to our house for dinner!" said Eric.

"Hooray!" cried the others.

With their trunks held high, the elephants led the way – walking calmly and very, **very** carefully!

89

Louis and Lisa Lion were just learning to pounce, and their dad had told them to practise as much as they could. So they were prowling through the jungle, looking for prey to pounce upon.

"There's something orange and blue and fluttery," whispered Lisa. "Here I go..."

POUNCE!

As Lisa pounced on the butterfly, Louis spotted something green and jumpy. He crept up and...

POUNCED!

Just then, Lisa caught a glimpse of black
and yellow fuzz. 'Perfect for pouncing,'
she thought. 'Ready, steady...'

POUNCE!

"OUCH!"

cried Lisa, rubbing
her nose with her paw.

96

"Maybe a bumblebee isn't such a good pouncing target! In fact, I think I've had enough pouncing practice for one day."

"Me too," said Louis. "Let's do something else."

But as the two little cubs bounded through the jungle, Louis suddenly saw a flash of orange and black in some bushes.

"A stripey snake!" he whispered. "It's too good to pass up!" So, at just the right moment, he...

POUNCED!

'OWWWOOWW!'

came a voice from the bush.
"What's got my tail?"

The 'snake' turned out to be attached to a stripey cub, just the same size as Louis and Lisa.

"Who are you?" they asked.

"I'm Timmy Tiger," said the little cub. "I've just moved here from The Other Side of the Jungle!"

"We're Louis and Lisa Lion," said Lisa. "Would you like to see what this side of the jungle looks like?"

Timmy said he would love to.

101

"Here's our river," said Louis proudly.

"It's nice," said Timmy, "but it's kind of small. Our river On The Other Side of the Jungle is as wide as fifty tall palm trees laid end to end!"

102

"Gosh!" said Louis and Lisa.

"And I can swim across that river – and back – without stopping once!" added Timmy.

"We can't even swim," said Lisa. "Will you show us how?"

"Err... maybe another time," said Timmy. "I'm just getting over the sniffles, and Mum said I shouldn't swim for a while."

A little farther along,
Louis and Lisa saw
Howard Hippo wallowing
merrily in the mud.

"Meet our new friend,
Timmy Tiger!" they called.

Howard opened his mouth in
a big grin. "Nice to meet
you!" he bellowed.

"Er... same here,"
said Timmy, keeping
his distance.

As the cubs scampered on, Timmy said, "On The Other Side of the Jungle, there's a hippo with a mouth as big as a cave."

"Really?" gasped Louis and Lisa.

"Yes," said Timmy. "Three tigers can sit in it!"

As the cubs walked on, something from a branch above dropped down in front of them. Timmy jumped, but Louis and Lisa smiled and said, "Hi, Seymour! Meet our new friend, Timmy Tiger."

"Greetingssss," hissed

Seymour snake. "Ssso nicce to make your aquaintancccce!"

"Nice to meet you, too," said Timmy, a little uncertainly.

"Well, ssso long," said Seymour,

as he slithered off.

"Sssssee you ssssoon I suppose!"

As Seymour slithered off, Timmy said, "On The Other Side of the Jungle, there are snakes as thick as tree trunks. Once, one of them swallowed me!"

"Oh, no!" cried Louis and Lisa.

"Yes," Timmy said, "but my dad hit the snake on the head and made him spit me out!"

"Really?" said Louis and Lisa, their eyes growing wider.

"Yes," said Timmy. "My dad's really, really strong, and he's twice as big as an elephant, and he can carry six gorillas on his back! And my mum can stand on her front paws and juggle coconuts with her hind legs, and... and..."

111

"...and what?" asked two smiling, normal-sized tigers on the path in front of them.

"...and, here they are," said Timmy, sheepishly. "Mum and Dad, meet my friends, Louis and Lisa."

"Happy to meet you," said Mr and Mrs Tiger.

"As you can see," Mrs Tiger added, "we are very ordinary and normal tigers."

112

"But what about all those amazing things Timmy told us?" asked Louis. "What about The Other Side of the Jungle?"

"It's just like this side," said Mr Tiger.

"So the river isn't as wide as fifty palm trees?" asked Lisa.

"And there's no hippo with a mouth as big as a cave, or a snake who swallowed Timmy?" asked Louis.

"No, indeed!" laughed Mrs Tiger.

Timmy looked embarrassed. "Well, they were good stories," he said.

"Yes," said Mrs Tiger,
"but they were just stories."
She turned to Louis and Lisa.
"Timmy had no friends to play
with in our old home, he spent
his time imagining amazing
adventures."

"But now that he's got friends like
you two to play with," said Mr
Tiger, "perhaps he'll have some
real adventures!"

114

"And there are more friends to meet, Timmy," Lisa said, "like Mickey and Maxine Monkey, and Chico Chimp!"

115

"You know, there are monkeys and chimps on The Other Side of the Jungle, too," said Timmy.

"Really?" said Lisa, glancing at her brother.

"Yes," said Timmy, "but I didn't know them. I can't wait to meet Mickey, Maxine and Chico!"

116

"Well, what are we waiting for?" said Louis, and they all raced off, ready for fun and excitement on *This Side* of the Jungle.

117

Fancy Flying

Penelope Parrot and her mum, Portia, were having a wonderful afternoon, watching the Fancy Flying Display Team. Penelope could hardly believe her eyes as she saw the birds swoop and speed through the sky, doing their amazing tricks and wonderful stunts.

That night,
Penelope dreamt about doing
magnificent stunts with the other birds...

...and, in the morning, she decided she would try to make her dream come true!

"I'm going to practise flying, Mum," she said. "I want to be the best!"

Before Portia could say a word, Penelope had zoomed off.

123

"The first thing I have to do is learn to fly really fast," Penelope told herself.

So she flapped her wings as hard as she could, to get up some speed.

124

But Penelope had only just learned to fly – so she didn't know how fast or how far she could go. Soon she was huffing and puffing and panting, and her wings were flopping instead of flapping!

"Oh, nooooo!"

she cried, as she felt herself falling

d
o
w
n,

d
o
w
n,

d
o
w
n,

until...

125

...SPLASH!

She landed right beside Howard Hippo, who had been enjoying his morning wallow.

"Gracious, Penelope," said Howard, trying to shake the water out of his eyes and ears. "You must be more careful!"

"Sorry, Howard," said Penelope. "I didn't plan that. I was just seeing how fast I could fly and my wings got tired. I want to be a Fancy Flyer!"

"Then you'll need expert help," said Howard.

"But I don't know any experts," said Penelope.

127

"But I do," came a voice from the bank.

"Mum!" cried Penelope. "How did you get here?"

"I followed you," said Portia. "I've got some special news. My uncle Percy has just arrived for a visit. He was a member of the original Fancy Flying team! He can give you the training you need."

128

Uncle Percy was delighted to
find out Penelope wanted to learn
to be a Fancy Flyer.

"I'll teach you lots of stunts first,"
he said, "and then we'll work on
one that will be your very own.
Every Fancy Flyer has a speciality!"

129

Uncle Percy and Penelope went right out to start her training programme.

"We'll begin with the Twisting Take Off," Uncle Percy said. "Watch me and do as I do."

"Now, straighten up and fly forward!" Percy called.

But Penelope couldn't stop spinning and spinning!

"WHOA!"

she shouted

"I'm getting dizzy Uncle Percy!"

Luckily, Penelope grabbed a branch
and managed to stop spinning.

Jeremy Giraffe, who was nibbling leaves nearby, helped Penelope up as Uncle Percy flew back.

"Never mind," said Uncle Percy. "You'll get the hang of it soon enough."

Just then, Penelope's friends, Mickey, Maxine and Chico, came swinging by.

"Want to play Mango-Catch with us?" they called.

"Great!" said Penelope, flying over to join them.

"Wait!" said Uncle Percy. "A Fancy Flyer in training can't waste her energy on games!"

"Sorry, Uncle Percy," said Penelope. "I guess I'll see you guys later," she said, a little sadly.

136

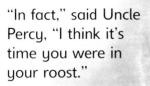

"In fact," said Uncle Percy, "I think it's time you were in your roost."

"But Uncle Percy," Penelope said, "it's so early!"

"A Fancy Flyer needs her sleep, my dear!" said Uncle Percy. "Those wing muscles need lots of rest to prepare for all the work they must do."

"Better do what Uncle Percy says," said Portia, as she helped Penelope settle on to her bedtime branch. "He's the expert!"

137

The next morning, Uncle Percy woke Penelope up very early.

"Time for your pre-dawn practice!" he squawked.

"But Uncle Percy, it's so early!" Penelope yawned. "The sun's not even up yet!"

"That's the best time to train!" said Uncle Percy. "Follow me!"

"We'll start with some speed exercises," Uncle Percy said. "This was my speciality when I was a Fancy Flyer. Just move in and out through the trees – like this!"

Penelope watched her Uncle weave gracefully through the jungle. It looked easy, but when she tried...

139

140

Uncle Percy came rushing back to look at Penelope's head.

"Nothing serious," he said. "A Fancy Flyer in training has to expect a few bumps and bruises! Best thing to do is keep going. Let's try it again."

All day, Uncle Percy tried to teach Penelope stunts. And all day, Penelope bashed...

...and crashed...

...and smashed...

...and splashed...

into trees, bushes, and other animals!

143

It was a very tired and worn-out Penelope,
who headed for home with Uncle Percy
that afternoon.

"Well, Penelope," said Portia, when the two arrived back, "are you ready to be a Fancy Flyer?"

"Oh, yes," said Penelope. "And I know exactly what my speciality will be!"

"What?" asked Portia and Uncle Percy together.

"Watching from the audience!" laughed Penelope.

145

Super Snakes

One morning, Seymour Snake's dad, Seymour Senior, said, "I have a surprise, son! Your cousin Sadie is coming to visit!"

"SSSensational!"

said Seymour. "We'll have so much fun playing together, just like we did when we were little!"

"Sadie may have changed a bit since you last saw her," said Seymour Senior. "She's been going to Madame Sylvia's Snake School."

"Oh, I'm sure she's still the same," said Seymour.

Later that day, Seymour slithered down the path to greet his cousin.

"Sadie!" cried Seymour. "It's so good to see you!"

"It's super to see you, too, Seymour," said Sadie.

"Come and meet my friends!" Seymour said eagerly. "You can play games with us, and..."

150

"Oh, I can't play games," Sadie interrupted. "Madame Sylvia always says, 'A well-behaved snake may slither and glide and wriggle and slide, but we DON'T swing or sway, or climb or play!'"

151

"You mean you don't climb trees?" asked Seymour.

"Certainly not!" said Sadie.

"And you don't swing from branches?" asked Seymour.

"Oh, no!" replied Sadie.

152

"Well, will you at least come and meet my friends?" Seymour asked hopefully.

"Oh course," said Sadie. "It would be rude not to!"

"HEY, SEYMOUR!" shouted Maxine Monkey. "Come and play Coconut Catch with Mickey and me!"

"Sure, guys!" said Seymour.

"By the way, this is my cousin Sadie."

154

"HI, SADIE!" shouted Mickey. Maxine and Mickey always shouted! "You can come and play, too."

"No, thank you," said Sadie. "I'll just watch. I don't swing or sway, or climb or play."

155

Sadie watched as Seymour climbed a tree, hooked his tail round a branch, and hung down with his mouth open. Mickey and Maxine threw coconuts for him to catch.

"It really is fun, Sadie," Seymour called to his cousin. "Are you sure you don't want to try?"

156

"It looks interesting," Sadie admitted, "but I don't think so. Thank you anyway."

157

The game had just finished when Penelope Parrot arrived. After Seymour had introduced her to Sadie, Penelope asked if they would help her practise her stunt flying.

"Sure, Penelope!"

said Seymour and he wound himself round the branch to make two loops.

158

WHOOOSH!

Penelope zoomed through the loops.

Seymour giggled as Penelope's feathers tickled him. Come up and try this, Sadie," he called. "It's fun!"

Sadie hesitated. "Er, maybe some other time," she said at last.

Seymour spent hours
hanging and swinging and
climbing — he even climbed
to the very top of a tree
to talk to Jeremy Giraffe.

160

Each time, Seymour invited Sadie to join him. And each time, Sadie looked more tempted – but she always said the same thing: "I mustn't swing or sway, or climb or play."

Later, Seymour spoke to his dad.

"I'm sure Sadie wants to play with me and my friends," he said. "But she insists on only watching. How can I get her to join in?"

"The only way," said Seymour Senior, "is to get Sadie to see for herself how much fun she could be having."

Suddenly, Seymour had an idea.

"Thanks, Dad," he said. "That's just what I'll do! See you later!"

"Where are you going, Seymour?" asked his dad.

"I've got to talk to some of my friends," said Seymour. "I'll be back soon." And he slithered swiftly away down the path.

The next morning, Sadie was showing Seymour how smoothly she could slide and how gracefully she could glide, when suddenly there was a cry of

"OH, NO!"

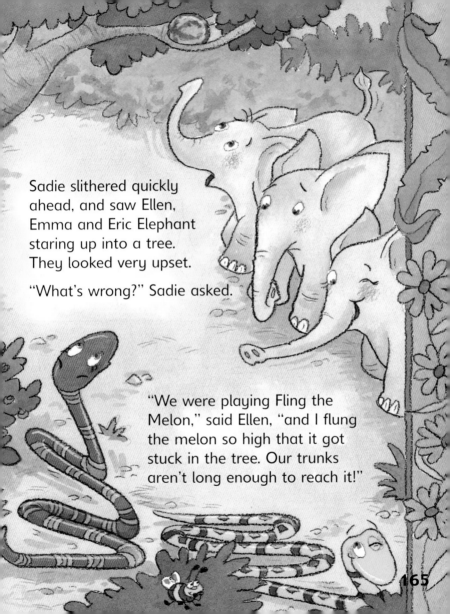

Sadie slithered quickly ahead, and saw Ellen, Emma and Eric Elephant staring up into a tree. They looked very upset.

"What's wrong?" Sadie asked.

"We were playing Fling the Melon," said Ellen, "and I flung the melon so high that it got stuck in the tree. Our trunks aren't long enough to reach it!"

165

"Oh, dear," said Sadie. "I'm sure Seymour will be happy to climb up and get it back for you. Won't you, Seymour? Seymour, where are you?"

Seymour had disappeared!

"Can't you help us, Sadie?" asked Emma.

"I'm sorry," said Sadie, "but I DON'T swing or sway..."

"...or climb or play," Emma finished. "We know about Madame Sylvia's rules. But didn't she also teach you that it's important to help others?" she asked.

"Well," said Sadie, "she did say that we must never pass up a chance to do a good deed."

"And this would be such a good deed!" said Eric. "We would be so grateful!"

"I'll do it!" Sadie decided.

Up Sadie went, winding round the trunk, weaving her way up into the branches, until she reached the melon at the very top.

"Here it comes!" she shouted to the elephants, giving the melon a shove with her nose. It fell straight down into Ellen's waiting trunk.

Thanks, Sadie!"
said Emma. "Are you
coming down now?"

"Er, not yet," said Sadie.

"I want to try something first."

With a quick wriggle, Sadie coiled
herself round the branch and
hung upside down above
the elephants.

169

"This is SSSTUPENDOUS!"

Sadie shouted. "I haven't had so much fun in years!"

She swung herself over to another tree, "WHEEEEEE!" she cried.

"I knew you'd enjoy this," said Seymour, slithering out from his hiding place. "You just had to try!"

"Come up, Seymour!" Sadie called.
"We can swing and sway together."

171

"Here I come, Sadie," said Seymour, whizzing up the tree. "But what will you tell Madame Sylvia when you go back to school?"

"I'll tell her," said Sadie, "that we MUST climb and play, and swing and sway – ALL DAY!"

To which Seymour and his friends could only add a loud

"Hip-hip-HOORAY!"

173

Snap Happy

One lazy morning, Claudia Crocodile was drifting down the river, looking for fun. Up ahead, she could see Mickey and Maxine Monkey and Chico Chimp playing on the riverbank.

"I think I'll give them a fright," decided Claudia. "It's always amusing to watch them run away!

Flashing and gnashing her sharp teeth,

she swam towards the three friends.

177

Sure enough, the

SNAP! SNAP! SNAP!

of Claudia's jaws scared the little monkeys.

"RUN," cried Maxine, "before she snaps our tails off!"

They tumbled over each other as they climbed to safety.

"Hee, hee!" Claudia laughed as she watched them. "Scaring the monkeys is such fun!"

That afternoon, Claudia
was bored again, so she looked
for someone else to frighten.

"Aha!" she said. "There's little
Timmy Tiger, paddling all by
himself. I'll give him a *real* fright!"
And she set off down the river,

SNAP-SNAP-SNAPPING

as she went.

180

Timmy didn't hear Claudia, until she was right
behind him! SNAP! SNAP! went her great big jaws.

GNASH! GNASH! GNASH!

went her sharp, pointy teeth.

" AAAAGGGGGHHH!"

screamed Timmy, as he saw Claudia's mouth
open wide. He tried to run away, but his paws
were stuck in the mud!

Claudia came closer and closer. Timmy trembled with terror.

"You're supposed to run away!" Claudia whispered.

"I c-c-can't," stammered Timmy. "I'm stuck!"

"Oh," said Claudia, disappointed. "It's no fun if you don't run away."

"Aren't you g-going to eat me?" gulped Timmy.

"EAT YOU?" roared Claudia. "Yuck! You're covered in fur! I prefer fish."

"Really?" said Timmy. "Then why are you always snapping and gnashing and frightening everyone?"

"Because that's what crocodiles do!" said Claudia. "We're supposed to be scary. Er... you won't tell anyone I didn't eat you, will you?" she asked, helping Timmy out of the mud.

"Don't worry," laughed Timmy, "I won't tell!"

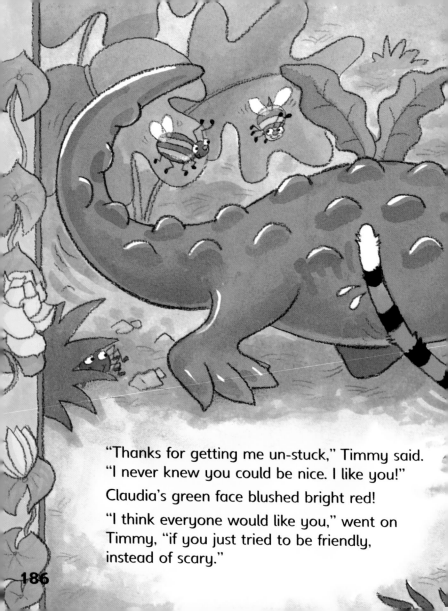

"Thanks for getting me un-stuck," Timmy said. "I never knew you could be nice. I like you!"

Claudia's green face blushed bright red!

"I think everyone would like you," went on Timmy, "if you just tried to be friendly, instead of scary."

"Oh, I don't think I can do that," said Claudia. "My jaws simply HAVE to snap and my teeth just MUST gnash! I can't help it."

"Wait!" said Timmy. "I think I know how you can be friendly and helpful and snap and gnash at the same time! Come with me."

As Timmy and Claudia went
along together, they saw Mickey
and Maxine trying to smash open
some coconuts.

"Here's your chance," Timmy
told Claudia.

Claudia nodded and swam towards the monkeys, her jaws

SNAP-SNAP-SNAPPING.

As soon as they heard her, the monkeys ran for the nearest tree.

"I just want to help," said Claudia, climbing on to the bank. "Throw me a coconut!"

The monkeys were uncertain, but Mickey tossed his coconut at Claudia's gaping jaw.

SNAP! SNAP! SNAP!

Quick as a flash, the coconut was open.

"Gosh, Claudia, thanks!" said an amazed Mickey.

Claudia opened Maxine's coconut, too. Soon everyone was sharing the cool, refreshing milk and chomping on chewy chunks of coconut.

Claudia had never shared anything before. She was surprised to find that she liked it!

"Hey, guys, look what I found!" called Chico Chimp, running towards his friends. He was carrying a big watermelon.

Suddenly, Chico spotted Claudia, whose jaw was open, ready to

SNAP!

"Uh-oh!" he gulped, turning to run.

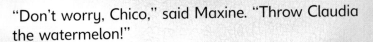

"Don't worry, Chico," said Maxine. "Throw Claudia the watermelon!"

Chico did, and watched in amazement as Claudia

SNAP- SNAP- SNAPPED!

the watermelon into neat slices for everyone.

"Thanks, Claudia!" they all chorused. Chico gave Claudia the biggest slice.

"Now let's have a seed-spitting contest!" said Claudia, and everyone cheered.

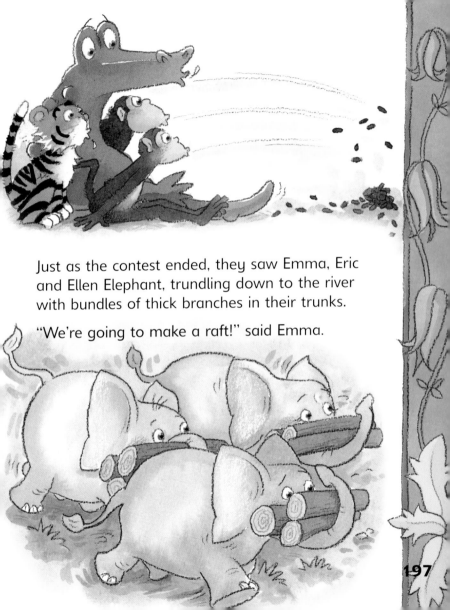

Just as the contest ended, they saw Emma, Eric and Ellen Elephant, trundling down to the river with bundles of thick branches in their trunks.

"We're going to make a raft!" said Emma.

"Yes," said Eric. "We just have to trim these branches... OH, NO! It's Claudia!"

As the elephants galloped away, Claudia went for the branches they had dropped.

SNAP! SNAP! GNASH! GNASH! went Claudia's strong jaws and sharp teeth.

"Wow! Thanks, Claudia!" said Emma, as the elephants came back. "That was really helpful!"

Claudia grinned. Being friendly and helpful was much nicer than she'd expected.

199

"Here we go!" shouted the elephants, when their raft was ready. The friends on the riverbank watched them.

"That looks like so much fun!" said Chico. "Can you help us make a raft, too, Claudia?"

"I can do even better," said Claudia. "Hop on my back!"

"WHEEE! This is GREAT!"
whooped Maxine
as they sailed down the river on Claudia's
back. They waved happily to the elephants
who waved their trunks back.

Happiest of all was Claudia, who had found
that having friends was much more fun
than scaring them!

201

Hippo's Holiday

It was a warm, sunny morning
in the jungle.

"A perfect time for a nice, long, relaxing wallow," thought Howard Hippo.

Wallowing in the river was Howard's favourite thing to do.

He found a nice, cool, muddy spot and settled in. Howard was just drifting off into a delightful daydream, when...

SPLASH!

"Gotcha!" shrieked Maxine Monkey.

SPLOOSH!

"Gotcha back!" shouted Chico Chimp.

206

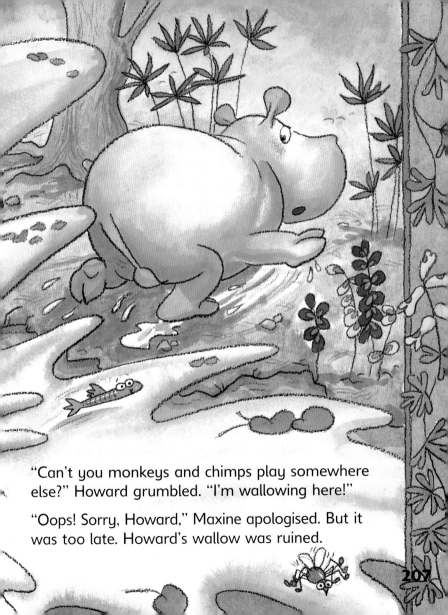

"Can't you monkeys and chimps play somewhere else?" Howard grumbled. "I'm wallowing here!"

"Oops! Sorry, Howard," Maxine apologised. But it was too late. Howard's wallow was ruined.

That afternoon, as the hot sun beat down on his back, Howard slithered into the river to cool off.

"Aaah," he breathed, as the cool water soaked his bottom. "This is soooo lovely."

"Yoo-hoo! Howard!"

called Penelope Parrot. "I've just learned to do a double-rollover-loop-the-loop! Want to see?"

"Sure, Penelope," sighed Howard. It didn't look as if he was going to have a chance to relax this afternoon, either!

The next morning, Howard's cousin, Hilary, came to visit.

"You look exhausted, Howard," she said.

"That's because I never have a chance to relax and wallow any more," said Howard.

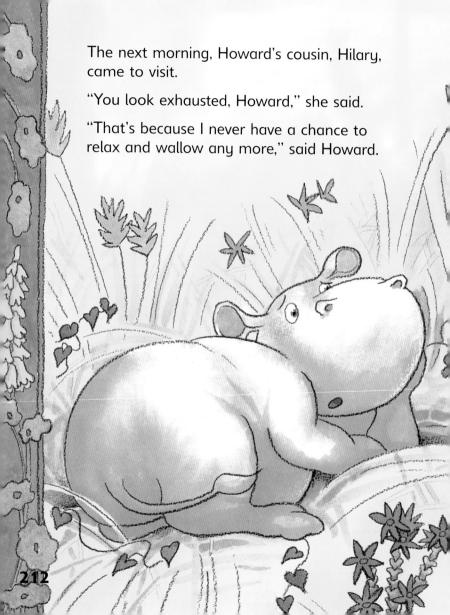

"What you need is a holiday," said Hilary.
"I'm leaving for Hippo Hollow this afternoon.
Why don't you come with me?"

"That sounds like a good idea!" said Howard.

213

"You'll love Hippo Hollow," said Hilary, as the two hippos trundled through the jungle. "There's so much mud!"

Howard saw himself relaxing in a cool mud bath.

"And there are streams and waterfalls!" continued Hilary.

Howard imagined having lots of cool showers.

"And everyone has lots and lots of FUN!" finished Hilary.

Howard thought about playing games with new hippo friends.

At last Howard and Hilary
arrived at Hippo Hollow.
It's even more beautiful than
I imagined!" Howard exclaimed.

"And it looks like we've arrived
just in time!" said Hilary.

"For what?" asked Howard.
"A relaxing mud bath?"

"No, silly!" laughed Hilary. "Hippo-robics!"

"Let's get moving, everyone!" called a sleek-looking hippo. Lots of other hippos galloped into the stream behind her.

"Come on, Howard," said Hilary. "Don't be a party pooper on the first day of your holiday!"

Howard had no choice but to join in.

"Kick, two, three, four!
"Kick, two, three, four!

shouted the instructor.

Howard did his best and kicked with all the others.

'Surely everyone will want a nice, long rest after all this exercise?' he thought.

But he was wrong! After a quick shower in the waterfall, everyone rushed off to play Volley-Melon and Hilary wanted Howard on her team.

219

Howard finally did get to have a rest after lunch – but not for long!

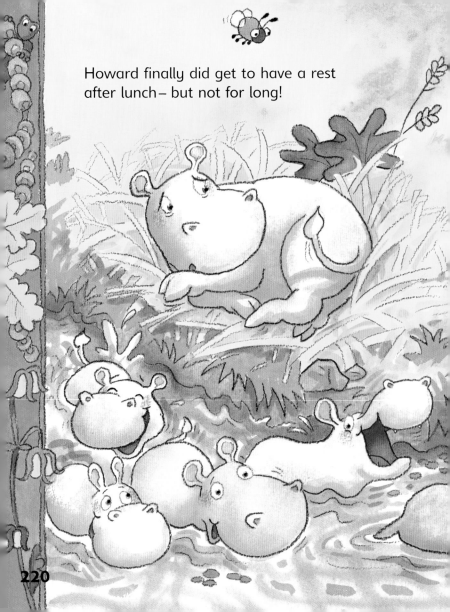

"You're looking much more relaxed, Howard," Hilary called, as she led her junior swimming class right past him. "This holiday was just what you needed, wasn't it?"

"Er... I guess so," Howard replied, weakly.

221

After his busy day, Howard was hoping for an early night. He was just getting settled, when he heard Hilary.

"Come on, Howard!" she bellowed. "You don't want to miss the Hippo-Hooray Cabaret!"

"They're good, aren't they?" said Hilary, as they watched the cabaret dancers.

"Oh – YAWN – wonderful," sighed Howard. He could barely keep his eyes open.

The next morning, Howard was sliding into the river, when he heard Hilary calling.

"Is it time for Hippo-robics?" he asked.

"Oh, no," said Hilary. "Lots of good, fresh air is what you need. So we're going on a hike!"

Howard huffed and puffed
all through the exhausting
hike. "I hope I can have a
nice cool bath when this
is over," he thought.

225

Howard got his wish. But, as he was soaking his sore muscles, Hilary came by for a chat.

"The hike was fun, wasn't it?" she said.

"Oh yes," said Howard. "In fact, I enjoyed it so much, that I've decided to go on another one!"

"Really?" said Hilary. "That's great! Where are you hiking to?"

"Home!" said Howard. "I'm going home, where I can have a REAL holiday – with no Hippo-robics, no Volley-Melon games, no cabarets and no one to stop me wallowing as long as I like!"

And that's just what
Howard did!

This is a Parragon Book
This edition published in 2004

Parragon
Queen Street House
4 Queen Street
Bath, BA1 1HE, UK

Created by The Complete Works
Written by Ronne Randall
Illustrated by Jaqueline East

ISBN 1-40542-643-8

Printed in China